THE EROTIC
PERCIPIENT
MIND

Lesbian Theme
Poetry and Prose

Saralle Ramson

outskirts
press

Outskirts Press, Inc.
http://www.outskirtspress.com

ISBN: 978-1-9772-2563-4

Outskirts Press and the "OP" logo are trademarks belonging to Outskirts Press, Inc.

PRINTED IN THE UNITED STATES OF AMERICA

Dedicated to the one who inspired My Passion.... Thank you.
I swim in your sea and I drown in your forever.

I am a hopeless romantic romancing the language of love

Saralle Ramson

The Want of You

There isn't much more I can say...there are no words left. Unafraid, I stand before you naked in all my vulnerability, giving you full access to the good, the bad, and the ugly of my truth. I have history in my baggage... moments of love as well as sadness, moments of pure joy and moments of devastation. I am not perfect. I make mistakes and am humbled by the circumstances I've lived that have nurtured the me I am today. So, here I stand in front of you... You, everything I've ever wanted in a woman... and I'm lost for the words that would create a meaning of how much I love you... your soul... your spirit... your mind. It is not for the want of your lips on mine or the warm touch of your stimulating hands caressing the heart of me that leave their mark on my memory... my want goes beyond the sensual attraction of your smile. And there are no words that suffice explanation... There isn't much more I can say.... There are no words left... there is only the want of you.

Saralle Ramson

I Don't Want to Rush

I don't want to rush... Your beauty is beyond the body that you hide to wear... or the hidden conversations your heart dares not speak... or the scars that healed the damage of your broken pieces of disillusionment. I don't want to rush... You are more than the lips that shower the essence of your passion on my skin... for I see more than the attraction of your wants... I see a less guarded soul. I do not want to rush... Every moment with you is so delectable. I want to savor your presence, licking my lips in its yearning, tasting the aroma you emit... but I do not want to rush. For the love that I feel is not measured by the appeal of your sensuality, but by the core of your simplicity and your truth. No, this is beyond special... I do not want to rush.

Saralle Ramson

On any given night when the breeze of its season brushes against my skin, it reminds me of you... and I smile. It's the same feeling I get when you touch me. Every fiber of my skin feels you... every moment breathes you. Alone in my thoughts, gazing at the night sky, I can't help but think about how your lips are all consuming like those stars, burning your kisses into my soul... I melt into them... and I smile at that thought. I breathe in the contentment, only to remember the aroma of your scent in the mist of ecstasy taking control of my memory....and I smile. Yes, smiling. I turn to go back in... let me get back to bed... and relive this memory in real time...

Saralle Ramson

I am not afraid of your pain or the excess baggage of sentiments that totes within it. I, too, carry scars. I understand yours. Let me touch your pain with the ache of my love for you, so that its light can lead the way out of your sadness into a world full of embrace and tenderness. Just open the door and let me in.

Saralle Ramson

Fuck, You're Fine.

You don't really know me and I don't really know you. You are a virtual imagination of the cyber kind, but it doesn't matter. You're still fine as fuck and I want so bad to get to know you in a way that the wireless connection can't ever provide. I want to experience your emotions in a first kiss. I want to feel your hands on my body, the sweet sweat of my skin on yours, nipple to nipple. I want to taste unimaginable lust that lays between your thighs...to feel the movement of your weight on me and dance to its intoxicating rhythm. In my imagination, you are that precious erotic dream...that euphoria, the ecstasy. I really don't know you, but, fuck, you're fine.

Saralle Ramson

Your insatiable lips made my chest move deeply and slowly with each breath I took. I felt my soul escape in your wants... I felt my wants escape to yours. I didn't feel the hands at the small of my back pushing me closer... closer to the smoothness of your skin, the warmth of your body, the beating of your heart, the touch of your lips, the aroma of your breath. I was wantingly lost in your savage kiss and your hands exploring the all of me... I can't think. There is only that insatiable kiss.

Saralle Ramson

The Gift

I giggle like a kid finding her own unwrapped birthday present hidden in a corner of the closet... only my gift is you. You. I found the gift of my lifetime... full of moments of intimate silences where only the deepest sighs are the breaths I dare take. I waited so long for this gift. Here you are. Real. I touch you with all the fragility of my own heart. Your tender embraces secure what is yours and I flow into the calming gift of the warmth of your skin. Your beauty dances about my desires. I am left with the erotic melody of your lips on mine. A whispering gasp of your name escapes from the depths of my orgasms. Delirium is your tongue wrapped like a ribbon on my ecstasy. The thought of you is euphoric. What a precious gift you are...A gift of lifetime.

Saralle Ramson

Underneath the Sheets

I felt your exploring hand underneath the sheets... it slowly awakened me to the touch of your fingers pinching the top of my soft panties and delicately sliding them off without any resistance. You feel the slender skin of my buttocks, thighs, and calves as my panties are tossed to the side. You get closer, spooning me as your hands makes its way back to cupping my nipple in your palm, covering the whole of my breast with your fingers. The warmth of your breath on my neck gives way to my sigh. I'm wide awake now, pushing myself closer, wanting more.

As your hand slides down my stomach, I feel your palm sensually arousing the pulsating throb of my clit that awaits the rhythm of your fingers. I'm drenched in wetness. I open to welcome them while your lips speak of the want of me... Ah, nothing compares to awakening surprises of morning delights and the feeling of your hand underneath the sheets.

Saralle Ramson

Just barely opening my eyes in the morning, the aroma of you still penetrates the air I breathe... lingers on the skin of my fingers... savors on the lips of my mouth and awakens my deepest wants to foreplay the morning hours away in the all essence of you.

Saralle Ramson

I thought about how comfortability ruins love. I surrender to that memory of where comfortability had not a chance to exist...a place where every conversation is new and when the excitement of hearing your voice captivates the wants that follow. I don't want to forget where your lips touched my soul...a place where you made me feel. I don't ever want to forget what it feels like to be in love with you, not for the moment, not through the years.... but for the rest of my living life. I never want to forget.

Saralle Ramson

I Read Her Words

I read her words as I sensualized each touch of my return lettered response of, I want you. The fleeting distance has faded the words I want to voice into a space of nothingness... where she hears only my silence, lost to the wires of void. But, I... I want to hear her soft breath. I want to see her alluring eyes. I want these fingertips caressingly touching her natural round breasts so lightly, so teasingly. I want to smell the aroma of her perfect lips in a fervent kiss where her own defenses melt into forgetfulness and she surrenders submissively to my explorations. Just give me an out of body experience, one moment, a moment where I can love her in all her nakedness and in all my desires... as if there were no tomorrows... only to want more. I read her deepest words. I felt her soul.... And all I could type was... I want you.

Saralle Ramson

Can you understand the depth of my fears if I didn't have you to love?

Can you understand the courage its takes to stand before you, naked and exposed?

Can you understand that I have destroyed my insecurities to merge with your safety?

Can you understand that there is no descriptive word to explain this intensity I'm feeling?

Can you understand that there is no meaning to my life without you in it?

Can you understand that I leave my heart in your hands so I can become part of your world?

Can you understand that I've fallen for you?

Saralle Ramson

She Doesn't Know

She doesn't know I see her through my wisdom heart. She emits a different kind of feel... a feel from another time, in another realm. I feel safe with her. When she touched my lips with hers, I tasted her intensity... it tasted deliriously familiar.... like home. At that moment, as her kisses devoured all my reservations, doubts, and self-made walls, I melted into her. She seeped flowingly within the orgasmic pulses that ran through my veins, her rhythmic movements pushing, her sensuality glowing, her all alluring. And as the curvature of her silhouette made her negligee dance on my body, her inviting hands captured my euphoria, and I close my eyes in ecstasy... because she doesn't know that I already see all of her beauty with my wisdom heart.

Saralle Ramson

My soul has not been the same since you entered it. I thought I knew what love is...all the things they say it is... "deep romantic attraction, an intense feeling of deep affection". At the core of the meaning, I feel so much more. How could I not see that the attraction is not just a magnetic pull... that its energy dances with my visual wants, leaving me drowning in erotic fantasies of dreams naked in you. Lustful dreams. The kind of dreams where you romance the tenderest wet part of me with your skillful lips... and I more than feel... I feel more than an intense feeling of deep. I moan with an energy that rushed up from the deepest part of my existence and exploded in all its sweet orgasm. I think my loving soul was touched by your beautiful heart and I haven't been the same since.

Saralle Ramson

You made love to me last night. I felt your tongue on my wet pussy... your hands on my butt. I moved with the rhythm your tongue was playing, strumming, flickering, swirling to its own beat... and I... shit, I'm drowning to the dance the moans make in my throat. Don't wake me up from this erotic dream.

Saralle Ramson

I'm so into you. You take my hand, guiding me to star gaze with you and the touch of your fingers entwine with mine profoundly seeps into my heart. The simplicity of the simplest of things as holding hands can be so deeply pulsating... you have to close your eyes and pause to take it all in. It is more than holding hands, more than an evening of star gazing... It is you. I'm so into you.

Saralle Ramson

When it comes to you, I accept that I lose my self-control... I lose it when my frenzy erotic thoughts take me to that moment when your fingers touched my back as you unsnapped my bra... when I feel you body pressing up against it, spooning me from behind, standing. Your hands fondle my exposed breasts as you massage the pinching of my erected nipples. I feel the full weight of your arms embrace me and the warmth of your breath as you kiss the side of my neck. I shiver to your soft whispers of love in my ear. The drunkenness of satisfaction consumes me into the submission of your foreplay. Yes, I submit. I submit to your every desire because I won't deny this feeling... this sultry want to lose my self-control... to surrender my soul, my heart, my love... when it comes to you.

Saralle Ramson

Romance

I want romance.

Play with it.

Dance with it.

Stay in love with it.

Take your fingers to the delicate pleasures of my skin...eat from me.

Dance your tongue to the places it desires.

Let the warmth of your body be the candlelight that lights my ecstasy.

Romance me and let's play in its mystery, get lost in its foreplay, and drink from its ocean.

Saralle Ramson

My Hunger

My hunger for you is insatiable. I want your morning delights, your afternoon surprises, your bedtime hours. I hunger for your silences, your humor, your seriousness.... your thoughts. I hunger for your life in mine.

My, My, My... I can't get enough. I feel a hunger that only you can satisfy....

I hunger for your smile and how your presence alters my everything.... an indescribable depth of a feeling... I'm at awe with it all. You leave me wanting more of you. Sometimes, I feel like I can't breathe.

I hunger for the flow your voice calls... calling me to your wants. I crave the moisture of your scrumptious lips as your breath relishes in the aroma of my quivering skin or when your tongue entwines itself in the wetness between my thighs and in the ecstasy of my orgasm... I'm left with only my moans that escape in my sighs. You swallow my essence whole.

Take me... give me your passion... for my hunger for you is insatiable.

Saralle Ramson

We Fall So Hard

We fall so hard when we love, don't we? It's hard to ignore the smiles on our faces and the happiness that stirs in our hearts... We cannot deny the sweetness of its warmth nor the pleasure of its passion. It quenches our urge for its thirst. It makes us yearn her enticing voice when she speaks to us in tones that unravels all our defenses, sometimes leaving us in a haze of stupor. But we don't care. It's such an amazing place to be.

In spite, that along with its complicated entanglement of anxious-ness at the want to see her, feel her presence, and touch every part of her essence, when we get to that moment... it is more than her body, her scent, her sensual sexuality that get to us. It's so much deeper than the skin that protects her. When we fall hard, there is a portal to the soul that reaches the epitome of our orgasmic ec-stasy... beyond the moans... beyond the euphoria.

Yes, as women, we fall so hard when we love. We see the woman that stands before us willing to let her nakedness speak to us.... to teasingly play the game of intimacy in our beds, on our couches, and in our soul. We see her varying natural moods that cause us to pause, to understand, and commit no judgement... because it is the woman in us that allows us to see more deeper at the courage it takes to give into love without the antagonizing fear of rejection. When we love... we fall hard, so hard. Don't we?

Saralle Ramson

Every day I awake to your smiles that are brighter than the radiant sun's warmth in midafternoon. They penetrate my shielded soul and sears my breakfast hunger into thoughts of morning delights. Your smiles say more than any words you can ever speak…. And that in itself is more than enough to make my world beam. -Sara Margarita Medina Ramos

Saralle Ramson

Por mi culpa. Because of my fault...I can blame only myself. I am guilty of losing my mind in the lust you offer. Bind me. Blind me. Tie me to your wants, your desire. I will not resist.

Por mi culpa. Because I take blame...I accept defeat. I surrender to this urging feeling to let your fingers explore more than the small of my back... to let your hand grab my neck, pulling me closer to you, demanding the meeting of our lips. I will not resist.

Por mi culpa. Because I am guilty...I apologize. I apologize for not having the courage to let you know how deeply I feel for you. It is because of my fault that I look at you from afar.

Por mi culpa. Because it's my fault...There is something about you that ravages my thoughts, moving the fireflies in my insides. I can feel the soft rasping of their wings and I cannot resist.

Por mi culpa, I will not resist the thought of you.

Saralle Ramson

I Adore You

I adore you...

My garden is yours to roam...

Touch it.

Breathe it.

Taste it.

Sacredly lose yourself in the nature of its scent.

Explore the path to euphoria.

Delight yourself in its succulence.

For I adore you...

And my garden is yours to roam.

Saralle Ramson

The Depth of You

With every sunset that soaks the horizon's blue
I fall deeper into the depth of you
The thirst of your passion surfs beneath my skin
When your fevered lips kiss my soul within
With every sunrise that greets the morning dew
I am filled with the gratefulness of you
For your fingers roam upon my wanting shores
Leaving love letters imprinted in my essence's core
With every starry night that glistens in the sky
The depth of you is captured through my loving eyes
Your shine and good energy beams in my heart
The beauty of your love leaving its mark
With every moonless night, the heavens speak to me
It tells me you're the one... the one who holds my peace
So, lay beside my soul, my love, and watch the world with me
The sunshine over the horizon, the sunsets on the seas
Let's star gaze the midnight sky, hold my hand entwined with yours
Let me rest my head on you, while your love is forevermore
The depth of you is all my heart can see
For our love is so attuned that it was meant to be
For our love is so attuned.... that it was meant to be

Saralle Ramson

There is something about you that draws me to your energy…your soul whispers its desire in unspoken words… and its message I fully understand. The universe is talking and I am listening. It brings me thoughts of you and a smile appears. The radiance of contentment that your world brings into mine is beyond understanding. It lights up my clarity, my vision, my feelings. I see all too clearly where this is leading… and I don't care. There is something so special about you.

Saralle Ramson

It's so easy to say I love you to you, because this, this what we have.... We have known always from our eternity past to the purpose of infinity.

Saralle Ramson

I have found someone who is turning my insides out with every thought I have of her.

Saralle Ramson

Her song seeps to the depth of my soul. My breaths are not my own... she plays my insides with just the music of her lips while her fingertips stroke the tune of my moans. It is an old vintage song from times of old not foretold.

Saralle Ramson

There is a feeling I can't shake off. A pressure in my chest. I feel you so. Is this what love really feels like? It gets in my throat as if I was to cry... no tears... no scream... Just this overwhelming energy of love that is so indescribable, my only option is to smile and absorb it. What is this? I've never felt this. All brought on by just your thought... Oh, my... I think I'm falling in love.

Saralle Ramson

Love when you find it and it fills you heart... doesn't matter the circumstances, your status, you mess... just love in the moment. Nothing else really matters.

Saralle Ramson

The horizon is where my ocean meets your stars.

Saralle Ramson

I've imagined every scenario, every look from those soft eyes, every thought before forethought about the aroma of your lips... I drown into a self-made memory. I'm a captive of your scent... that deliriously intoxicating scent I've imagined as you make love to me in my dreams. I've imagined every scenario...Everything.

Saralle Ramson

I can say "I love you" a million times the depth of what I feel and it wouldn't even come close to the magnitude of the pressure my insides feel when I'm without you. My all is so into you... that words need not be spoken. But "I love you" is what whispers out my soul when the heart cannot contain its delirium.

Saralle Ramson

I feel the thoughts of her dripping onto my black panty, her tongue outlining what I submit her to take. I open wider. Yes, she knows the spot... As my erected clit pulses to her rhythm, my hands clutch her mane, holding on as if dancing to her mouth's ravage taste of me....and I...well, I silently sigh at my thighs ability to tense towards orgasm in such a public place.

Saralle Ramson

You are the light of my day, showering me with the rays of your powerful love... an unimpeded intensity that burns the desires of your wants into blood pulses under my skin. My days will never be the same since you have shared this bed. Your soft alluring whispers of good morning while our heads have barely left the comfort of our pillows, have made sure of that and your loving kiss on my forehead has cemented the delirium of my reality. I am blinded by the brightness of your soul... intoxicated by its beauty. It warms my mornings and I am eternally grateful, my love.

Saralle Ramson

I want to feel you every day for the rest of my life as if it were the first time I said "I love you".

Saralle Ramson

I look at your hands and I fantasize... you are My Passion

Saralle Ramson

Soulmate

Sleep, my lady, dream
My soul lays at your side
She kisses your forehead softly
To bless your thoughts tonight

Sleep, my lady, dream
My heart lays at your breast
She pleasures from your breathings
To soothe your calming rest

Sleep, my lady, dream
My body wants you so
She soaks in your wanting
She wanders in your abode

Sleep, my lady, dream
My all sleeps with you
I cuddle your desires
As I await your morning due

Saralle Ramson

There in your hands lay
My Embrace,
My Heart,
My Love,
My All

Saralle Ramson

The Song of You

The song of you fills the wants that satiate my every thought. I am captivated by the chemistry of your lips as it savors my erotic moans... that rhythmic pleasure that escapes when I lose control under your spell. Dance with me under the stars with your thoughts... Let the moonlight stroke me with the touch of your hands. The night breeze breathes of you. Come. Sing your ecstasy into me... for I am a fool...madly in love with you.

Saralle Ramson

The Blank Sheet

The blank sheet stares at me. It calls for the pen-stroke of my mind... the secret desires unwritten... already satisfied by your wanderings in my erotic fantasies. But how to spell the deepest love of the way you move me with your voice? Or the humor subtleties that make me laugh and lights up my smile? What meaningful word can portray the orgasmic moans when you eat me? When your tongue has its way? When your hands flame the passion into my wetness?

When your lips devour my control and leave me exhaustingly pleased? This blank sheet just stares at me. With pen in hand, I stop... I have no clue, because I want so badly to get to you.

Saralle Ramson

Pull Me In

You pull me. Your hand grabs my lower back drawing me closer. So close, I feel your breath on my neck, and I become one with the beat that gives you life. You pull me tighter to your hold. I won't struggle. Your touch is like a magnet. I can't resist its pull... I flow within it. I am flushed with your warmth and the exhuming sighs of contentment we both share in the moment. Your strength excites me, but your gentleness assures me. Oh, my God... the want of your lips as they slowly near mine makes me shiver. I'm consumed by the scent of your breath. Time is at a standstill. Your love leaves me defenseless and in delirium. There is nothing more I can do... I surrender. Yes, baby.... whatever you want. Pull me in.

Saralle Ramson

I thought of you again... there is no normalcy to it. It's a dirty erotic thought. Your hands entwined with mine... the weight of your body between my legs... the rhythm of your thrusts... the savageness of your mouth... your erotic whispers between your breaths, leaving me aroused, wet, and screaming your name.... damn, woman.... I thought of you again.

Saralle Ramson

From Across the Room

I watch you from across the room before your eyes caught mine. One split second to salivate in minutes of curiosity. I smiled... how dare you undress me with those eyes... so deliciously bold. My tongue tangos with the outline of my lips, teasing before taking a sip from my Chardonnay. I watch you watch me leave burgundy lipstick marks on my glass. I reciprocate your stare... My blinking sensually slow. What makes you think that I'm not undressing you?... from across the room.

Saralle Ramson

The poet of my soul speaks of you. It is mesmerized by the sensuality of your energy that pens its thoughts deep onto my forethought. Come to me, it says. Let me sooth in the warmth of your arms. Let me lay onto your cinnamon skin like the palm tree's shade in the sand. Let me dress you with my wants...and undress the nakedness of your desires at the shores of mine. Let me swim in your waters... for your essence voices its presence in thought and the poet of my soul needs to speak of you.

Saralle Ramson

I want to touch your mind...the part that holds the mystery to your madness. I want to move in the thoughts you entertain... hidden in secret. Hypnotize me with the sensuality of your feminine deity... take me to the warm flow of your lips as it captures the savors of all that it wants from my body. Take me to your hands...exploring the wetness of my full bloomed flower. Do not fear my presence. My piece of mind will cuddle into the home of your soul.

Saralle Ramson

Imagine This

Imagine this... I'm cooking. The aroma of the "Sofrito", a mixed sauce of blended sweet peppers, "culantro", (a Puerto Rican version of cilantro), garlic, tomatoes and onions basting in a little bit of olive oil, fills the kitchen with the marinating simmer of ground beef I'm preparing for my homemade chili. Hm, it smells so good in here. Just as I am lowering the heat, you sneak from behind without my notice. Your surprised embrace catches me off guard and I step back onto you... I close my eyes as your lips explore the curve of my neck. You know, hon, it's my weakness... your breath on my skin. Like the savoring air that looms in the kitchen, I am deeply breathing the sweetness of you. I breathe the calmness before the storm... and I feel the heat before the thunder. As your hands slip underneath my black and snugged tank top, you grab my breasts... your eagle spread fingers seizing the wholeness of them as you proceed to feel the erection of my protruding nipples. You stay to foreplay in my arousal, taking full advantage that I don't wear bras while at home. I know, babe.... I'm a tease that way and you respond so lovingly. You're wanting dessert before dinner. No problem. No waiting... I'll serve that right up, mi amor. Imagine this... I'm cooking... Hope in my weakness to submit, I don't burn our dinner.

Saralle Ramson

To Satisfy Your Lips

There is nothing more I would want than to satisfy your lips with my yearning's plea... undress me, piece by piece. Let me feel your hands lightly touch the nerves that make my skin respond with shivery as you slip off my clothes. Your hands... your hands artfully create the mood like a brush on my canvas. You paint your desires with my moans. The subtleness of your caress, yet the intensity of your savageness consumes the ecstasy of my euphoria and I clutch the sheets as you taste the wetness of my orgasms. Your lips...Yes, I want nothing more than to satisfy your lips.

Saralle Ramson

Your Voice

There is an echo of a call in my memory commanding me at will. What am I supposed to do with this magnetism? You call me with whispers on my skin like the ocean's breeze riding the mist of crashing waves. Your voice, elegant in its ravage, yet thunderous in its beauty... like water, clear and transparent, you flow within me with every word your lips form. I close my eyes. That is what you do, honey... when I hear your hypnotic voice electrify the very element of my existence... just by saying, "Hi, babe".

Saralle Ramson

When I think of you, damn, all I can do is smile. It's the funny moments that replay in my mind over and over. Makes me want to come over and just hold that happiness in my arms forever. There are also those special moments that fill my heart with love uncontained. I want to kiss you. I want to tell you all the feelings words really can't say. I want to hold you even if it's but for a moment... I want the all of you... When I think of you, damn... all I can do is smile.

Saralle Ramson

A Very Good Thing

As I dwell on my tummy flab, the wrinkles, the hair color change... the elasticity of my skin... it is difficult to focus on what if anything is good about ageing. But your comforting words of love overshadows any self-ego perception that my thoughts might want to sabotage. I thought I had lost my youth in this skin. I thought I lost all the attractiveness of my adolescence years that drove my sexual promiscuity. I thought I lost my energy. Yet, your words of adoration thrusts deeply within me, bringing the full luster of my sensuality to a fruition, making me feel alive. I feel so alive. I respond to your advances. Your voice pulls me into to you. My skin reacts to the gentle touch of your hands... because they are your hands. Your lips drink the chemistry of my needs because you know how to turn me on. Your breath between my thighs creates its own memory. And I.... I think about the taste of you long after we've made love. I may dwell on all the aspects that make me dread getting older, but one thing is certain... your propensity to satisfy my every desire is as strong as the very first time you showed me what love is... and that alone distracts me. I forget that I'm ageing and that is a very good thing.

Saralle Ramson

I couldn't sleep last night. Why? You ask... I was filled with you.

Your dreams.

Your thoughts.

Your pain.

I couldn't sleep last night

Saralle Ramson

I Wish It Were That Simple

I wish it were that simple... to forget your touch for a moment. Then I could breathe... breathe between my thoughts. But your fingers stroll the avenues of my pleasures with such purpose... my neck, my breasts, my thighs, my prize... there is no moment I wish to forget.

I wish it were that simple... to forget your lips for a moment. Then I could think... think between the delirium of my clarity. But your aroma sends me relishing in its allure... on my neck, my nipples, my naval, my orgasm... and again, there is no moment I wish to forget.

I wish it were that simple... to forget your voice for a moment. Then I could move... move between the melody tones of your whispers. But your sound is one that hypnotizes... my mind, my soul, my heart... and there is no moment I wish to forget.

I wish it were that simple...

Saralle Ramson

Have you ever felt a feeling so deep and without thought that it il-luminates your smile with a glow of love... and you knew instantly who touched you in that way?

Saralle Ramson

Once Upon a Time

Once upon a time I fell in love with the unexpected. From the first time I saw you standing there, something happened. You talked through my soul... and I was afraid, yet.... I welcomed it. Afraid because of how I felt... the deep force of a strong ache, yet.... a calm. It had a sense of home. I understand it now. My continual yearning to be close to you and when I do.... it smells like home. When your skin plays with mine.... It touches home. Once upon a time I fell in love and the most beautiful thing about it is that I continue to fall with each passing day... unafraid.

Saralle Ramson

Let's Not Think About Tomorrow

Let's not think about tomorrow, my love.

Just give me this moment....

A moment to wine my lips with the taste of yours

A moment to emboss my skin in your thoughts

A moment to hold you for eternity

Just give me this moment...

Let's not think about tomorrow

Saralle Ramson

I'm over my head in you, drowning in my own restless wants. Your lips engulf such a mesmerized appeal. I watch them move in slow motion as they whisper their intent... and my yearning for them pulls me deeper into the depth of your lust. I am drenched in the love that devours my self-control. You occupy the breaths that I take. There is no getting over you... when I'm over my head in you.

Saralle Ramson

I Ache

I ache for the touch of you...to let my fingertips trace the curvature of your womanhood, to feel your skin's reaction as it arches its back.

I ache for your lips... to dwell in them while they sigh, breathing me into the salacious thirst of words unspoken.

I ache for the taste of you... your river overflows with the movement of my tongue and I savagely feed upon it... its aroma savors the air I breathe.

I ache for the moments... those incredible moments where I've lost myself in the euphoria of your delirium and find myself in its truth as we become one.

This craving, this lust, this feeling of wants... leaves me love struck....
I ache.

I ache for the want of you.

Saralle Ramson

From a Distance

From a distance, I can see you want of me. Your wants show in your eyes, but it is your lips that move and your soul that speaks... I want to take in all of you.

From a distance, I can feel your want of me. It caresses the pleasure between my thighs, its hands know no bounds... I'm wet before you touch me.

From a distance, I can taste your want of me. It savors between your lips and feeds me its passion... I'm already delirious.

From a distance, I can imagine anything I want. From a distance

Saralle Ramson

Breathed Your Breath

The first time we kissed, I breathed your breath... I floated on its whispers. I closed my eyes to its depth. My deep sighs moaned in the pleasure of it. Your aroma converged on my lips at the touch of yours and I drifted into a state of euphoria like I've never known... never felt before... Can't get you out of my head, woman. That is what you did the first time I breathed your breath.

Saralle Ramson

You're Beautiful

I know you are not used to hearing these words... but, honey, honestly...you're beautiful.

I want my nipples to warm your back while you sleep

I want my mound to rest on your butt, cuddling in spooning

I want my hand to caress your breasts to gently wake your smiles

I want my breath to touch your neck into welcoming a new day.

You're beautiful. I want to wrap myself in your awe.

Saralle Ramson

You have become my world and I want to travel every inch of you.

Saralle Ramson

Let Me Kiss Your Lips

Let me kiss your lips and feel your heart beat on my chest... Let me hold your neck tenderly as you wrap your arms around me... I want to feel your warmth... I want to smell your aroma... I want to melt into your passion. Let me kiss your lips

Saralle Ramson

If time were mine, I'd give you my eternity...

Saralle Ramson

The Bathroom

You slip into the tub and it's your time to yourself... your space... to soak in the warmth of waters that soothes your tired day... to close your eyes to the peace it bathes you in... to dwell in the thoughts that make you smile. In that solitude of thought, where nothing or no one can disturb the fantasies that roam in your secrets, I desire to be.

Do as you will in your daydreams... in your afternoon pleasures, or in your evening hour thoughts.... but think of me. Think of my hands massaging the suds on your back. Think of me as my nails glide lightly on your skin. Think of me when you are caressing the soap that clings to your breasts as if my fingers were fondling your nipples and my hands were grabbing their fullness.

You slip into the tub and it's your time to yourself... your space... but, in the solitude of your thoughts in the bathroom, it becomes mine.

Saralle Ramson

Every time I see you, I can't explain the urgency of my hunger. Is it your smile or the lips that accentuate the sensuality of them that moves me to kiss you? Every time I see you, my insides quiver... the sensing of you emanates from the pulse in my veins. I feel my skin hot at the thought of you. I have no defense. Is it your mouth on mine, the passion of your scent on my lips or your probing wandering fingers spreading my thighs... the result of playful foreplay that leads you to the wetness between them? Your thirst quells my hunger. I taste euphoria. Every time I see you, I can't explain this urgent... hungry feeling.

Saralle Ramson

In order to sleep this tired soul, I imagined you holding me in your arms as I felt the nipples of your breasts on my back move to the deep breaths of your dreams. I felt the warmth of your spooning and I settled into its calm. You have a way of calming my soul just by the thought of your embracing love. I fell asleep with your presence. It was as if I needed to dream of you.

Saralle Ramson

Look at Me

Look at me. I stand before you naked and insecure of my beauty. My breasts are yours to fondle... my lips for you to kiss... my body for your fingers to explore. These treasures I gift to only you. Yet, I am nervous and anxious. My legs tremble... my heart races... my thoughts occupied with the all of you. In my own wants, I am a captive... the want to breathe you in... to exhale in the moans of pleasure when you thirst between my thighs or when you surface to share your hunger on my lips.

Yes, I stand naked and insecure of my beauty. But, look at me... your tenderness draws me closer and I am unafraid... unafraid to let go of my fears... unafraid to allow you in.

Saralle Ramson

How many times have you made me smile not so innocently...

Saralle Ramson

Your Forever Lover

You are my poetry... the words flow effortlessly because I feel your love. I can touch it with my thoughts... you are always on my mind.

I am afraid of losing it... the poetry you instill in my heart. I want time to stand still, yet, I want to move on into you love.

Never in my dreams would I have thought I'd fall in love so deeply that for once I wouldn't mind losing myself in you.

You make me feel alive. You make me feel loved and appreciated. You make me feel so woman.

Up to now, I thought I knew what love is, how it felt. I was wrong. This feeling is new. It's deep. It consumes my all.

It has nothing to do with sex or its appeal. It has everything to do with a soulful connection of electrifying energy.

I want to touch your most inner source. I want to walk by your side. I want to la in your silence. I want to kiss your forehead.

I want to be your forever lover...

Saralle Ramson

Her Magnetism

What do you want from a relationship? I don't mean expect. Expectation is someone else's standard. An expectation that no one can really maintain because it's an illusion... a perfect example of placed conditions on a relationship yearning for the unconditional... wrapped with pass lessons learned, and a pretty bow to disguise everything you don't want.

What we don't want is obvious. Our past experiences have burned into us the reality of our mistakes... scaring our ability to trust our own decisions. What makes us happy isn't so cut and dry, though we've made of list of exactly what we don't want in our lover. We are concerned more in all that has hurt us, but have paused to consider what happiness truly means to you in a relationship? We are all complicated women and have learned the art of concealment... even within our own desires of happiness.

So, what do you want in a woman? Each of us have our own vision of what that may be. It cannot be expressed in One-liners... or even a story. Do you know why? Because love's magical energy is a magnet. You have set perimeters to protect yourself from hurt and in doing so, you have blocked energy's flow. You just haven't been pulled so hard where you levitate into its magnetism.

What I want in a woman is her energy... her magnetism.

What do you want in a Woman?

Saralle Ramson

I Can Get Used to This

I can get used to this... the look you give me that turns me on... that look that always follows with a I love you... the way you hold me in your arms... comfort and intimacy in silent moments. How I love that peacefulness.

I can get use to this...the tone of your voice when you say my name... the movement of your lips at the touch of mine... the whispers in between breaths that leave me craving. Your aroma invigorates my senses.

I can get use to this... the way you don't rush... where your mouth slowly tastes every inch of me... my neck, my nipples, the fullness of my breasts... my wetness. You devour my moans.

I can get use to this... the way your tongue uses my body as its playground... where I immerse into its erotic frenzy... where you drown in my delirium... only to start again.

Yes, I can get used to this.

Saralle Ramson

When It's Right

When it's right, it's so right. You finish my thoughts as if we were one. Get out of my head, woman, but, then again, I'd climb out of my skin to be in yours because as one, we could conquer the world... My sanctuary is your home. I know no other place.

How deep can my love be? ... As deep in the abyss of my soul where my wants of you cry from joy. My breath comes from your exhales. Your heart's unspoken whispers calm me as I lay my dreams on your chest. I know no other voice.

Your intimacy goes beyond our silences... your kindness... the little things you do with intention that puts a smile on my face and that mean the world to me. This deep ache of happiness dwells in my spirit. But I know no other feeling.

When it's right, it's so right. Our paths, journeys, distance, all had a say in this moment, in this time, in this place... here, where everything is right... I know no other life.

When it's right, it's so right. -Saralle Ramson

The Music of Your Soul

Romance me with the music of your soul and let your heart take my hand as we dance to the rhythm of its truth.

Saralle Ramson

Your hand slipped underneath my soft silky panty...your fingers warmly fondled my clit, touching my essence. I let you spread my legs as I sigh a gasp and my breathing deepens with the tenderness of your lips on my neck. My thighs tense. Woman, I have no control in resisting nor do I want to. I'm yours.

Saralle Ramos

Unquenchable

There, beyond the spell of your beauty, lays the essence of my wants... the wonders of your lips when you smile... the effect of your sultry voice that incites the wetness between my thighs... and the warmth of your touch at the slightest graze. I long for your presence.

You are more than the enticing conversations of smiles and laughter... the subtle niceties of pleasantries... and the calmness you bring to my world of chaos and madness when I feel too stressed.

In every moment, my thoughts are of you... this connection... the awe of it all.

I just want you to know... my want of you is unquenchable.

Saralle Ramson

You are a raindrop filled with the simplicity of love that falls deeply into the essence of my soul... my heart has thirsted a lifetime for you and my mind an eternity.

Saralle Ramson

A Figure of Your Imagination

I don't want to be a figure of your imagination. I want to walk into your reality and touch you... Feel your lips on mine... feel my hands on you.

This urge is too real to let it slide by the wayside. I feel like the crashing waves on your sandy shore... repeatedly wanting the taste of you... coming back for more... I want more than to be a thought. I want to be your desired memory... not a dream, but a life.

I don't want to be a figure of your imagination.

Saralle Ramson

Dear Universe,

How many times must you put me through circumstances to show me what love really feels like? What have I not learned that when it is at hand... I, for the moment, can't have it? Is it the comfortability you've shown me that you want me to accept? The wants of my passion have been shelved. Do you want it exchanged for the mundane art of racing to the edge of death? I resist. Must I always be the vessel to show others the kindness of caring while losing the fire of love and intimacy of that love to time? Must I live by this void of acceptance of the cards you've dealt me? Must my being be a sacrifice of happiness for the destiny of another? And how does knowing all this that you have laid before me... give me the option to walk away from someone I use to love, but now only the utmost caring resides? How can I walk away when they are in need...? and you have put me exactly where you need me to be. Shall I resist? Or shall I trust your plan?

Saralle Ramson

Enough for Me to Smile

You make me smile more when I see you laugh at my silliness or the feeling of contentment you give me when I'm with you. It just adds to the affirmations of the deep connection that we both feel... in our conversations and in the understanding of our thoughts even in moments of silence that seems to find a home in our minds. But, then again, everything about you makes me smile... when you brush your hair back with your hand, the way you grab your naked breasts to tease me, unexpectedly catching me off guard, the thought of you soaking in the tub... or the thought of you trying to sneak into my shower... of course I pretend to not to have noticed... all of it a turn on that just lights me up.

The everyday of mundane living that others may have doesn't exist for me. There is a difference between settling in routine and finding moments that take my breath away in the small details of attention that we share between us. It takes me to another place where, frankly, my eyes cannot get enough of you... my lips sigh in the moisture of your mouth... my thighs tremble at the touch of your hand and I give of myself freely. And with just the thought that I am so in love with you... I smile. With just the thought that this calm, this immense feeling of being wanted and loved, is enough... it is enough for me to smile...even more than seeing you laugh... even more than the happiness we share. You are enough for me to smile.

Saralle Ramson

I Love How You Love Me

I love how you love me... like the softness of your lips in the places that make me moan your name or the feeling of your chin as it rocks to the rhythm of your tongue between my thighs. The scent of your mouth on mine after they've had their fill devours my sighs, leaving me breathless. The bedroom sheets have my grasping fingermarks on them... my pillow dented from my head's tilt... your wandering fingers exploring the wetness it finds as you begin again, returning to fondle my erected nipples... your hands, your, lips, your mouth cup and play. There is only you, your whispers, your touch and the weight of you taking command. The night has no time as the moon watches and hears the howling deep breaths we both take. The chemistry is unreal. I want to scream from my pores... I love how you love me.

Saralle Ramson

I Feel at Home

Your captivating voice of good night sings lullabies that ease me into sweet dreams of you. Is it possible to love someone so deeply... even in sleep the want lingers? The weight of your arm around my waist... your breath on my neck... the pounding of your heartbeat on my back... your thighs...how I love the feel of them as they warm me. Our bed holds a multitude of memories, moments that fill me intensely with your wants of me and mine of you. The pillows feel the grip of my hands with fervor. The walls hear the ecstasy of our passion. In the hustle of life, it is that moment when night falls that the intimacy of you reminds me of why I love you so. My heart smiles and I fall into your calm... the calm of us. I feel at home under the covers with you.

Saralle Ramos

The Hem of My Black Negligee

I feel the hem of my black negligee caress, oh... so lightly on the mid part of my thigh as I walk towards you. Your eyes, absorbed in my every movement, cause my nipples to erect and protrude through the silkiness of my gown. Your look does that to me. I'm physically touched by your gaze. Your wanting eyes... where I'm undressed before your hands remove my panties... That calming chaotic place... where I can see your lips call me to foreplay inside its kiss... where the bed you lay invites me for company as your lover. The bed that has my fingerprints on its headboard... where your mouth has its fill of me... where at nights end, underneath the covers, my nightgown and panties lay crumbled and forgotten. That calming chaotic place where I feel the hem of my black silk negligee.

Saralle Ramson

I Don't Ask for Much

I just want a woman who gets me. Someone who sees how complicated I can be, yet so satisfied with the simple things in life. Touch me now and then with tenderness that makes me shiver. Embrace me with your wants and desires. Devour me into your savored kisses. Let me feel your warmth. Show me how much in love you are without words and that you're as happy as I feel... that what we have is the real thing because... because I am so in love with you. I don't ask for much... I don't ask for much.

Saralle Ramson

CPSIA information can be obtained
at www.ICGtesting.com
Printed in the USA
LVHW030320240520
656396LV00007B/671